Go, Go, Go!

Kids on the Move

Stephen R. Swinburne

BOYDS MILLS PRESS
An Imprint of Highlights
Honesdale, Pennsylvania

Introduction

Let's say you wake up at seven in the morning and fall asleep between eight and nine at night. That means you're awake about fourteen hours of the day.

For most of those fourteen hours, your day is full of activity. You may start your day by hopping out of bed. After breakfast you jump on the school bus or go skipping off to school. You chase your friends around the schoolyard or run with the basketball. In gym class you might stand on your head or swing on a rope. At recess you cartwheel or climb or piggyback.

And when you get home from school, after a snack and homework, it seems like you have to get moving. You may ride your bike or splash under the fountain or go sliding at the playground.

When dinner is finished and night comes, you may spend your last ounce of energy bouncing on the bed. And when your head finally drops on the pillow, your body will tell you how busy you've been. Before you fall asleep, think about all the ways you moved today and what fun ways you might be on the go, go, go tomorrow.

Steve Swinburne

What's your favorite way to move?

I walk.

I skip.

I hop.

I run.

I twirl.

I roll.

I swing.

I dance.

I jump.

I piggyback.

I sled.

I ski.

I balance.

I bounce.

I cartwheel.

I climb.

Did you ever slide
with a friend?

Did you ever fall
into the leaves?

Do you like to ride a bike?

Or ride a horse?

Do you follow the leader?

Or stand on
your head?

Have you gone slow in the mud?

Or fast on a slide?

Monkeys like to hang. Do you?

Dolphins like to splash. Do you?

It's time to reach for the sky.

Let's go, go, go!

To all those kids on the move out there and to all those parents and teachers out there who have said a million times, "Where do they get their energy?"

—*SRS*

Acknowledgments

So many people helped me in making the photographs for this book. To all those adults who pitched in and corralled the kids and to all those kids who kept on smiling and kept on the go, huge thanks. I wish I could thank individually every child, teacher, and parent who contributed, but I've not enough space. Two school districts in New York City were an especially big help: School District 27 in Queens and School District 31 in Staten Island.

I'd also like to thank the kids and teachers of Brattleboro Central School, Brattleboro, Vermont; Flood Brook Union School, Londonderry, Vermont; and the Northwest Elementary School, Rutland, Vermont. Special thanks to my daughters, Hayley and Devon Swinburne, and my nieces, Jessica DiPardo, Elina and Melody Swinburne. Thanks also to Rudi and Cameron MacKugler.

Cover photo: Keith Johnson (left), Lucy Bolognese (middle), Andrew Gayda (right)

Boyds Mills Press, Inc.
815 Church Street
Honesdale, Pennsylvania 18431
Printed in the United States

The Library of Congress has cataloged the hardcover edition of this book as follows:

Library of Congress Cataloging-in-Publication Data

Swinburne, Stephen R.
Go, go, go! : kids on the move / written and photographed by Stephen R. Swinburne. —1st ed.
[32] p. : col. photos. ; cm.
Summary: A photo essay of children in motion.
ISBN: 1-59078-022-1
1. Motion—Fiction—Juvenile literature. 2. Children—Pictorial works.
(1. Motion—Fiction. 2. Children.) I. Title.
[E] 21 AC CIP 2002
2001099218
Paperback ISBN: 978-1-59078-038-1

First paperback edition
The text of this book is set in Garamond Book.

20 19 18 17 16 15 14 13